GRANDMA'S SPACE ADVENTURES

Book 2

Donna Colangelo

ISBN

RIDDLES

Answers throughout the book.

What **milk** can you not drink?

What **hands** cannot clap?

What **novel** cannot be read?

Activity

FIND 5 DIFFERENCES

FIND 5 DIFFERENCES

Find 8 differences

Find 10 differences

Contents

Chapter 1

"Grandma's here! Grandma's here! Grandma, did you bring your spaceship? How long are you staying with us?" Blair and Jake shouted joyfully.

"Boys, it is so great to see you! I've missed all five of you. I left the spaceship at Grandma Joannes. I'm planning to stay for about three days. Are there any more questions?" replied Grandma.

Next, the boys discussed who Grandma was going to sleep with. It was a tough decision.

Finally, Grandma decided that one night with each boy would work out perfectly. The boys, after a lot of space inquiries, finally fell asleep. With the boys sound asleep, Grandma could talk to Charlie and Kelly about taking them on the spaceship trip. It was their turn to explore the outer space.

Grandma told them about her two space trips. Kimberly's friends Nonna, Nonno, Glen, Michelle, Avery, and Cathy joined Grandma on her very first trip. It was fun.

Joanne's family Christmas trip with her three children and grandson. We picked up a ghost on that trip, so taking the ghost home will be Grandma's third trip.

Grandma reminded them that all she needed was three successful trips before they would allow her to take the boys on a space trip.

A long silence filled the room. Everybody was thinking deeply.

Grandma broke the silence by suggesting that they, Kelly, and Charlie discuss it.

Grandma went into the kitchen and busied herself making tea until their conversation ended. Bringing in the tea, she asked them how their discussion went and what they had decided.

"Do they need to prepare a safe trip party or not?" Grandma asked.

"Okay, start the party Mom, but one of us will go with you!" Kelly announced with a smile.

"You have made your old mother very happy and given her a thrill," Grandma said while hugging Kelly and, later, Charlie. "There still remains the ghost return trip," Grandma told them before going to bed.

Grandma enjoyed three days with her amazing grandsons. Then left for Joannes' to go on the return-the-ghost trip.

Continuation Book 1 Chapter 5

Book 2

Chapter 2

Grandma was getting depressed without her spaceship. There was not much to do. She took her garden chair and a cup of coffee to sit and stare at her spaceship for some time.

Grandma had a strange feeling something was watching her. Maybe a ghost?

“I just want to go home.”

“Who said that?” asked Grandma in a surprise.

“Your friendly ghost.” The voice answered.

“Where is your home?” Grandma asked the voice.

“The exact place where you hit my invisible ship.”

“So, that happened in reality. We will take you back, friendly ghost. Don’t worry about it.” Grandma replied. She was glad to have some answers.

Wade, Courtney, Cody, and Grandma headed out. They left Mason and Joanne's home to be safe and to look after the dogs.

The ghost was quiet until it saw its family and friends. "Stop, my friends are all there, waiting for my return."

The ghost said that they had surrounded the spaceship, which made Courtney and Grandma nervous. There were more ghosts around.

"Okay, Mr. Ghost, now please leave our ship," Grandma said firmly.

"No, we want your ship. We are not leaving." The voices of all the ghosts replied.

Grandma said, "No, how will they get home without a spaceship?"

Wade said that he had a feeling something was going to happen. He and Cody had discussed how it could be a trap, so they came prepared.

"You can keep your spaceship to get home, but you must give us the girl." The voice replied again.

Courtney's eyes were as big as a saucer.

"Don't worry, Grandma will not let that happen."

"Thanks, Grandma." Courtney replied.

"WADE, CODY!" Courtney was waiting for their reassurance.

"Okay, we won't let them take you. We can't go home without Courtney. We cannot get home without my spaceship." Grandma said. She was very frustrated.

"So, what are we going to do?" Cody asked.

Wade answered, "I thought of this, so Cody and I installed a shield that makes us invisible."

Wade told the ghost to leave now. After the ghost was gone he put the invisible shields up.

Cody had installed guns that popped out when the shield was lowered. He told them to lower their shields so they could send them the girl.

Courtney fainted.

With both shields down, Cody had installed a projector, so he projected a picture of Courtney. While they were looking at what they thought was Courtney, Cody had the guns pointed at them just in case they attacked. Wade took off as fast as the spaceship would go. They put the shield up again.

Courtney woke up when they took off.

The ghosts, realizing that it was just a projection of Courtney, took off after them. Because the visible shield was up, they got away. Cody not able to see the invisible ghosts fired the guns rambled to scared the ghost.

Courtney was jumping up and down, and she ran around hugging everyone. They managed to save both the spaceship and Courtney! Great success.

Still invisible, they got home and parked the spaceship in the same spot in Joanne's backyard. They took a break and stayed in the spacecraft for a few days. Once again, Tickles and Oreo were running in circles, barking at the invisible spaceship.

Joanne was puzzled. What was happening? They were laughing at the dogs. When Joanne came outside to check on the dogs, she heard them laughing and ran into the house, screaming. She was on the phone with a realtor when the whole gang walked in. Courtney was still laughing when she told her mom the whole story of her close encounter.

"Thank God you didn't let them have Courtney." She was thankful to them.

Chapter 3

After the safe trip party, Grandma loaded the spaceship. Grandma, with Uncle Don, Charlie, and her four Grandchildren, were on their way.

Exploring the universe is exciting and amazing.

Charlie, the boy's dad, and Uncle Don were working on their space license, so Grandma let them take turns co-piloting the spaceship. Charlie was sitting up front with Zen on his lap.

Grandma was busy driving the spaceship and dodging asteroids.

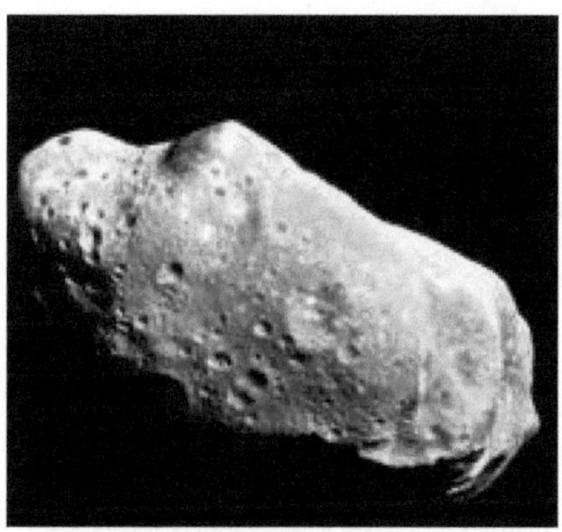

Asteroids, sometimes called minor planets, are rocky remnants left over from the early formation of our solar system about 4.6 billion years ago.

Uncle Don was playing games with Jake, Blair, and Emma.

When young Zen shouted, “Uncle Don, LOOK, LOOK. OVER HERE!” Everyone ran to look out the window. A climbing wall and a fire truck with its ladder extended were on a planet.

Uncle Don and Zen, both serious climbers, were jumping up and down, saying, “Let’s go down!!!! Let’s go down!!!”

Grandma guided the spaceship smoothly down. Uncle Don and Zen were the first out of the spaceship. They ran straight to the climbing equipment. Uncle Don was halfway up the climbing wall, and Grandma, Emma, Blair, Jake, and Charlie were still getting out of the spaceship. Zen was climbing the fire truck ladder. They were both in their glory.

Charlie, Grandma, Jake, Blair, and Emma (non-climbers) walked to the planet's middle. There, they saw children with bent legs and sad faces.

The climbing equipment caused their bent legs. The parents looked sad because their children could no longer run and play. Charlie, a doctor, got started on fixing the children's legs. Everyone was pleased with the outcome.

The parents were dancing and smiling when Charlie finished straightening all the children's legs.

Suddenly, the fire truck, with Zen swinging from the ladder, comes roaring by. It's sirens screaming.

There was a baby dragon suck in a tree. Because it was scared, it was blowing small amounts of fire.

Jake was steering the fire truck, and Blair was working the gas peddles. Emma was working the sirens.

They were going to rescue the baby dragon.

The next thing they saw was Zen petting the little dragon, and the dragon was licking his face.

Charlie's face turned completely white; he was in shock. Uncle Don grabbed and shook him out of his trance.

Before firemen Blair and Jake can get out of the truck, Uncle Don is climbing the ladder to get Zen and the dragon.

All were saved, and they brought the baby dragon back to the townspeople. They rejected the baby, knowing the mother dragon would follow right behind them. Sure enough, down flew the mother dragon, breathing fire. Jake and Blair run out with the fire hose and put out the dragon's fire.

Meanwhile, little Emma had made friends with the baby dragon and refused to let it go back to the mother.

Then suddenly, the sky darkened. Bolts of lightning shot out of the sky and down about 2 feet (0.61 m) apart. The boys run for shelter, forgetting Emma and the baby dragon. The mother dragon watched.

The mother dragon flew down, grabbed Emma and the

baby in her claws, and flew off.

Everyone was in shock; Grandma was crying, and the men were pacing, trying to figure out what to do. Everybody was scared and stressed.

In the distance, they could hear Emma singing and the baby dragon howling. Everyone was relieved to hear from Emma. The singing and howling kept getting louder and louder.

Grandma said, “If they keep this up, the mother will bring them back.” She had no longer finished stating the fact and the noise stopped.

Everyone looked up, and there was the mother dragon bringing back Emma and all the children she had taken. It was a relief to see.

There was dancing in the street and cheering by the parents. Our little Emma was a town hero.

Blair said, “Boy, my mom was wrong screaming and loud singing does reap the rewards.” The people were laughing and cheering all of them.

The parents invited them to a celebration dinner.

Grandma told everyone to smile and eat no matter what they served. Everyone was sitting at a long table. When the food came out, it looked disgusting. But they all smiled and rubbed their tummies. The parents grabbed the food and left in a hurry. Leaving everyone totally confused, and not knowing what to do or say.

A young boy came out and asked how they could hate the food without even trying it.

They did not realize that they had offended the parents. The boy explained that smiling meant dislike, and rubbing the tummy meant a hurricane was coming. Putting on their frowning and sad faces showed that they were ready to eat.

This time, when the parents bought the food out, they all sat down and ate together. The food was different, edible if you didn’t look at it. They got into the parents' good grace, and the parents insisted on giving Grandma a recipe for beagle juice. Grandma was thankful, but she knew she would never find the ingredients. Grandma gave them a recipe for bran muffins, knowing they would never find the ingredients.

Jake had found a piece of the dragon’s lightning bolt. He carefully examined it. There was no electric charge in them. He took it to the parents to show them there was no electrical charge. Everyone cheered at the sight of it.

It was time for everyone to head home.

Jake bought a piece of lightning back home with him. When he got home, he went out to the dessert and set the lighting down. After about 5 minutes, the lighting show started—word spread.

Every Sunday, Jake holds a lighting show. Jake studied every performance—light without electricity. Grandma was sure Jake would figure it out.

Chapter 4

Grandma and the children's hairdresser, Renee, joined us on our next adventure. Jake, Blair, Zen, and Emma enjoyed having a fresh face to talk to. Jake, the scientist, showed Renee all his books from past trips. Blair talked her ear off, telling her about our past trip. Emma explained how she got her pink nose in the book Emma's Unicorn Story. Zen gave her his cute smiles and lots of hugs and kisses.

Everyone relaxed and enjoyed the view of the Milky Way.

The Milky Way is the galaxy that includes the Solar System, with the name describing the galaxy's appearance from Earth: a hazy band of light seen in the night sky formed from stars that cannot be individually distinguished by the naked eye.

Renee, hearing of past trips, was excited about this adventure.

Renee was showing the boys different styles on Emma's long hair. Emma was thrilled, and the boys were pretending to be interested. Grandma was proud of the children's behaviour.

After a few days and many hairstyles, Renee shouted, "STOP THE SPACESHIP! STOP IT RIGHT NOW!"

She saw a planet with trees made of hair. How could trees grow hair instead of leaves? Grandma explained that anything is possible in outer space.

They landed the spaceship and walked through the forest of hair. Each tree was a different colour and shape. It was a beautiful scene.

Zen, who loved to climb, started to climb a tree.

It shook and cried out, "STOP."

Everyone stopped immediately. They realized that they were not trees but living beings. Actual real living beings.

Renee took out a pair of scissors from her emergency bag. She started to cut their hair when the ground shook and the sky darkened.

A loud voice shouted: "STOP."

Grandma asked, "Who do you think you are, and why

should we listen to you?"

"I am KING PONYTAIL, King of this planet, and you must leave now." roared King Ponytail.

"I think we should leave that up to the hair trees. If they want a tree trim, I will be doing it." Renee answered. She continued, "I will NOT leave until I do what the trees want me to do."

Renee took out her scissors. The ground shook again, and all but Renee grew hair till the whole group was covered in hair. Renee started to cut Grandma's hair, but it grew faster than she could cut it.

Renee thought for days what she should do and why her hair did not grow. Then it hit her; she had scissors in her hand. She gave Grandma a pair of scissors and started to cut her hair. It did not start growing back. Everyone cheered. The hair began to grow back when she took the scissors back.

Now, that is a problem, as Renee only had seven pairs of scissors. She started by handing the group scissors and cutting their hair.

Renee cherished the first pair of scissors that her mom had given her. The scissors brought back many memories of her childhood and hairdressing school days. She did not wish to part with them. But she saw a little girl and decided she couldn't leave her looking like a hair tree. With a tear in her eye, she gave the little girl her cherished scissors.

“WOW, WOW!”

The little girl multiplied the scissors. She handed Renee her cherished scissors back. She had enough scissors to supply all the trees. Our tiny tree had solved the problem.

Renee thanked the little tree and trimmed her hair. “Wait till I tell everyone at the beauty salon about my tree-trimming experience,” announced Renee.

Renee thought she had died and gone to heaven. She started to cut and cut and cut. They put on the music, and the dancing began. There was so much hair they made pillows with it.

Renee became exhausted and had hand cramps. She could no longer trim trees. Renee felt she could return to tree haircutting after a day’s rest. Everyone returned to the spaceship for a refreshing meal and a good night's sleep.

No one noticed the large tree that had sprung up overnight.

Renee’s hand had improved, but she would have to take hand breaks. They were visiting with the freshly trimmed beings and listening to their history when “King Ponytail” entered the picture.

The people had all gone bald from head lice, beetles, and all the pollution. King Pony gave us hair if we would let him be their King. They gave him their loyalty. Then, he started to make demands that couldn't be fulfilled. He got meaner and meaner. He wanted to take the children away from the parents.

Renee stated that every time they said no, he would make our hair grow. Then he just couldn't stop, and we ended up covered in hair and unable to walk.

After listening to their story and a good night's sleep, Renee returned to trim more people's hair. She later found out that a lot of scissors were missing. The people that Renee had cut yesterday were crying, for they were worried that everyone would blame them. She knew they were truthful, as she had watched The Behavioural Panel on TV. They could tell those who were lying by their body language.

Blair pointed out the new colossal tree that was not there yesterday.

Just then, the colossal tree turned into King Ponytail; he had the missing scissors in his hands. He flew away, laughing horribly.

Now, Renee could not trim those that lacked scissors.

The tiny tree could not make more and cried because she did not make extras. Everyone comforted her and said, "Do not worry, we will devise a solution."

Everybody put on their thinking hat. Grandma, being the senior, had more life experience. After a few minutes, Grandma jumped up and down, singing I know I know!

Grandma took charge; everybody find a partner. Now, stand close to each other. Grandma walked down the rows just in front of Renee. Grandma put a pair of scissors on each tree's branch.

Renee got back to trimming.

Jake and Blair worked on cutting the hair to the waist. Emma and Zen played in the hair while stuffing the hair into pillowcases.

Grandma cut to the neck, and Renee did the rest.

The only problem was they had to stay together as partners and carry a pair of scissors.

Grandma was scouting the planet when she saw a pole with strings tied around it. She called for the people to come and see what she had found.

Tired of carrying scissors, they cut all the strings that led out to the sky. They heard a pop and King Ponytail crying as he floated away.

Renee was lifted on the men's shoulders and carried around the planet. Everyone was dancing and celebrating their new stunning look. She was a real hero for them.

The people gave her a group picture, all smiling.

Then, the time came for the group to leave. With lots of hugs, kisses, and tears, they headed to the spaceships. Grandma was looking in the mirror, stating it was her best cut in 70 years.

They partied, celebrating their new haircuts all the way home. We exited the spaceship looking our finest. Family and friends were happy to see them. Everyone was glad to be home. Renee became famous and opened her own Beauty Salon called The Hair Loft.

Chapter 5

Grandma loaded the spaceship with her new generator and other necessary supplies; she was ready to go. The Trimbles were all ready and totally excited to go.

Grandma Emma and Grandpa Ron Trimble were nervous. Grandma showed them her space license from the Canadian Space Agency and NASA. Reid, their grandson, with his guitar, and Pepper, his dog, were giving the spaceship a thorough inspection. Grandma thanked Reid for his inspection and his go-ahead.

Reid had brought his dog, Pepper. He stated that it was a good thing Grandma had left her dog, Tickle, at home. Pepper could make Tickle sneezy. Grandma said, "You've got a great sense of humour. Mr. Reid.

Dan, Reid's dad, is a pilot, so as co-pilot, Grandma did an excellent launch. There is not much difference between a space license and a pilot license. It is much easier if you have both.

It was snowing, which lit up the sky. Only the space junkyard could ruin it. Grandma explained to the Trimbles how much it upset her. They have to hold the billionaires and the government accountable.

Emma, Ron, and Grandma were teaching Reid Bridge.

Reid caught on quickly. Reid's dad, Dan, his mother, Joan, and his sister, Sierra, were watching and learning.

Grandma said, "They could always play bridge at home, so put the cards away, and everyone directs their attention to space."

Reid was still a big fan of Jurassic Park movies. Hence, all of us were on the lookout for a dinosaur planet.

Looking out the window, Grandma saw a planet with a vast ocean. She put in the coordinates, hoping to find it on future trips.

They spotted a planet with an enormous jungle. Grandma lowered the spaceship to get a closer look when suddenly, the face of a Dilophosaurus peeped in the window. Reid was jumping up and down, shouting, "IT IS A DILOPHOSAURUS!"

They all went silent for about 30 seconds, and then all of us spoke at once, saying, "They never heard of that dinosaur."

Dilophosaurus is a genus of theropod dinosaurs that lived in what is now North America during the Early Jurassic, about 186 million years ago. Reid informed us that they do not spray venom, and they do not have an expandable neck frill.

They use their tail as a weapon.

Dilophosaurus was a fast-moving, meat-eating dinosaur. A kink in its upper jaw may mean that it ate a certain kind of food or attacked by gripping and holding on to prey - modern crocodiles have a similar kink.

They are also bigger than they appeared in Jurassic Park. Remember that they have a weak jaw and are carnivores. I couldn't remember if a carnivore was a meat eater or a plant eater. Reid was nice enough to inform that it was a meat eater.

Grandma informed Reid that they would not be going down there. “Please, let's go down,” Reid begged.

Joan said, “I don’t think so!!!”

“OH, OH, Mom, Dad, there is an **Archaeopteryx**.”

Archaeopteryx differed from other birds because it had teeth, a flat sternum, a bony tail, belly ribs, and claws on its wings.

“NO, Reid, it’s not happening.” reinforced Dan.

They circled the planet and ended up right overhead, a beautiful lake with lots of beaches. They spent the night hovering over the planet. In the morning, they felt like they were in a trance, looking at the beauty of the planet’s lakes, flowers, trees, and beaches.

There was no sign of the dinosaurs. Or so they thought. Sierra suggested they take the time off from our travels and spend a day at the beach. The hot sand and cool water were just too tempting,

Grandma landed close to the lake, just in case they needed a quick exit. They played in the sand and swam in the clear blue water.

While they were sunning themselves and dozing off, an enormous shadow came over them.

The shadow belongs to a huge, beautiful, massive **Archaeopteryx.**

They rolled under the spaceship. Where they had put the picnic bag for safekeeping, they quickly piled the sand high around them.

Grandpa Ron packed it down tight. Only their heads were sticking out the top.

The Archaeopteryx tried to stick its head under the spaceship and got its mouth full of sand. Choking and making a really strange noise. It turned and flew away.

Unfortunately, the **Dilophosaurus** heard the ruckus and came pouncing down the beach.

"Grandpa Ron, did you get those Ex-Lax pills?" Asked Grandma Emma

"Yes, they were on sale, so I picked up ten packs. They are in the lunch bag," replied Grandpa Ron.

"Okay, everyone, take the sandwich meat out of the sandwiches. Wrap the Ex-Lax in the meat and throw them at the dinosaur." Grandma Emma ordered.

The dinosaur fell for it and ate all of them. After about one minute, we heard a loud rumbling sound.

Sierra shouted, "It is thunder."

Then a tremendous bang and the dinosaur rolled on its back and moaned. It got up and did an enormous poop.

They were killing themselves laughing when they heard rustling in the grass. They dug their way out from under the spaceship.

"Let's get out of here fast," shouted Grandma as she ran around and into the spaceship.

They all escaped into the spaceship. Grandma couldn't fire up the rockets. They were full of sand. In a flash, Glen opened the hatch and was out cleaning the sand out of the rockets. He had just got in and closed the hatch when they heard a thump on the top of the spaceship.

There is an **Archaeopteryx** sitting on the top of their spaceship. It was clawing at the window!! The whole spaceship was shaking more than they were. A lot of praying was going on.

Joan, a firefighter, suggested we electorate it. Grandma said that she had a feeling they would need a generator.

Reid played his guitar to calm down both beast and man.

Dan thought they needed to wire the generator to its claws. Everyone looked at Reid's guitar. Unfortunately, they had to use Reid's guitar strings for the wires.

Dan and Joan went about constructing a gadget for the wires. The window opening was limited. So, the gadget had to be smaller. The wires had to reach the beast, stick to the beast, and then they could apply the charge. After a few tries, they felt they had one that would work. Now, they require something to glue the wires to the beast. They searched the entire spaceship for some glue.

Sierra shouted, "Hooray for me. I have nail glue."

So, they applied the nail glue to the tips of the wires. Joan opened the window and guided the stiff wires out the window and on top of the spaceship. They waited a few minutes, and the beast stepped on the wires.

Reid and Sierra counted to three, and Grandpa Ron pressed the generator's start button. Goodbye, beast!!!

They started the rockets, and as they were lifting off, they saw the **Dilophosaurus** eating the fried **Archaeopteryx**. Now, they were homeward-bound.

Chapter 6

Okay, Mom, you can take Jake along with Auntie Jackie and myself for a trip on your spaceship. They can leave in a week. I have to get everything ready for the other two boys. Blair was very mad at both of us. I'm sure he will get over it. Kelly, tell him I will take him, with Uncle Don and dad Charlie, on the next trip.

Well, the spaceship was all packed and ready to go. Kelly, Jackie, and Jake loaded their van and headed to Airdrie for their space travel. They had a farewell party, which was a success, as Auntie Joanne and dog Oreo showed us their dance moves. The rest of us were learning the new moves.

Grandma, Kelly, Jackie, and Jake headed out on a rainy day. The rain made our launch even more challenging, but Kelly and Jackie managed to stay calm. The rain threw us in a whole new direction.

The sky was gorgeous. Whirling colours, sprinkling stars, and fireworks lit up the sky.

Right in this beautiful universe was a small, dark, lonely planet. Jake, the scientist, needed to discover why there was a difference. He decided they should go down and investigate the planet. Jake always needed to investigate the unknown.

The spaceship landed. Kelly, Jackie, and Jake let Grandma stay on the spaceship to read and rest.

Grandma was worried but didn't show it. This planet was too dark and scary for her liking. When they landed, they walked around shouting hello, hello. No one answered. The planet was uninhabited. They believed they were safe.

Jake spotted the great, big, beautiful science lab first. Jake got to work studying the planet's soil and atmosphere.

Kelly and Jackie explored the planet and found some interesting facts. They found some white mountains. They went back to the spaceship and got their coats.

Walking back to the lab, Kelly tripped and fell into a crater. Jackie was right behind her.

They opened their eyes and saw some aggressive fox-looking beasts. They attacked Kelly and Jackie. In her fear, Jackie did jumping jacks. The creatures stopped, looked at Jackie, and then followed her out of the crater, doing jumping jacks. Kelly followed all of them, doing jumping jacks.

When they got to the surface, Jackie, Kelly, and the adoring fan club did jumping jacks right up to Jake's lab.

"Mom, I didn't know you could do jumping jacks, and what are you doing with these beasts?" Jake asked.

"They are called Kangox, after kangaroos and foxes," replied Kelly.

The name impressed Jake, and he laughed back to the business of the Kangox.

"Jake, we can't stop doing jumping jacks, or they will

attack us. So, your mom and I are taking turns doing jumping jacks," said Aunt Jackie.

The Kangox joined right in, doing jumping jacks. After a period of time Kelly and Aunt Jackie grew very tired. Kelly grew tired, and her jumping slowed right down. It was becoming obvious that the Kingox were getting bored. Jake was watching all of them, and they looked so sleepy that he began to sing a lullaby. This put even Aunt Jackie and Kelly fast asleep. Jake woke Kelly and Jackie, and they tiptoed away from the Kangox.

When further away from the Kangox, Jake, Aunt Jackie, and Kelly hurried back to the spaceship. Kelly told Jake that she was sorry she ruined his exploration.

"No problem, Mom, I was finished. I got all the information I needed. I got soil samples and a bottle of the atmosphere." said Jake.

Thinking they were out of harm, they had some coffee and celebrated their escape.

Meanwhile, some of the Kangoxes had surrounded the spaceship, blocking the rockets so they couldn't leave.

Now what? They all looked out the window and growled at the Kangox. The Kangoxes laughed at them and made fun of them by laughing and doing jumping jacks.

Jake thought if he laughed back at them, they might leave.

It did not work. They kept blocking the spaceship.

This was becoming a no-laughing matter. They growled showing their massive teeth, and they were showing that they were ready to attack. They pressed their faces up against the window and rocked the spaceship. They were barking at us; no more nice Kangoxes. Oh no! That was bad news!

Aunt Jackie and Kelly crawled down the rockets, laid flat on the ground and put a net around them. The Kangoxes just hopped right over the net.

Okay, they knew they needed a better plan. So, the girls went back up the rockets and into the spaceship. Grandma stopped her reading, looked at the girls and Jake, and asked them one question.

"Okay, boy and girls, what are foxes and kangaroos afraid of?" Grandma asked.

Grandma was raised on the prairies in Canada, so she knew all about foxes.

The Canadian Prairies is a region in Western Canada. It includes the Canadian portion of the Great Plains and the Prairie provinces, namely Alberta, Saskatchewan, and Manitoba. These provinces are partially covered by grasslands, plains, and lowlands, mostly in the southern regions.

Grandma told them that foxes are afraid of flashing lights and loud noises, spraying them with water and throwing things at them.

Jake said he knew about kangaroos. He said he had been to the kangaroo farm in Kelowna, B.C., Canada.

Kangaroos use their strong tails for balance while jumping. They are the tallest of all marsupials, standing over 6 feet tall. Kangaroos live in Eastern Australia. They live in small groups called troops or herds ("mobs" by Australians), typically made up of 50 or more animals.

Jake said he had read that kangaroos were afraid of dingos.

Grandma said, “Here is the plan. When I count to three and say go. Kelly, you are in charge of the spaceship’s outside lights. On command, you will flash them on and off. Aunt Jack is in charge of the noise. On command, you will turn on the radio as loud as it will go.

Jake, you are in charge of the dingo noise. On command, you will bark loudly like a dingo. Okay, is everyone ready?”

1 2 3 GO!!!!!!

It worked like a charm. The kangoxes were out of their way in a flash. Grandma was patting everyone on the back and cheering.

Everyone found all this to be hilarious. They then relaxed, had dinner, and went to bed.

Jake shared his fascinating findings. The sad little planet was Pluto. Jake explained that The International Astronomical Union (IAU) downgraded the status of Pluto to that of a dwarf planet because it did not meet the three criteria the IAU uses to define a full-sized planet.

Essentially, Pluto meets all the criteria except one.—It “has not cleared its neighbouring region of other objects.”

Grandma said, “Jake is not only intelligent but knowledgeable.”

Everyone felt sorry for Pluto, and they decided to make it shine. They covered it with sprinkles, rainbows, and gummy bears. You could tell that Pluto was happy as he was turning faster than usual.

They all flew home feeling good about this adventure. They were glad to be back on earth—family and friends were there to greet them.

When they got home, Jake informed the astronomy world that he had found Pluto. Using telescopes and with Jake’s instructions, they found Pluto. Pluto was back in the astronomy books. They were all pretty pleased with themselves.

www.ingramcontent.com/pod-product-compliance
Lightning Source LLC
LaVergne TN
LVHW052301100826
845147LV00001B/109

* 9 7 8 1 9 6 3 7 4 6 0 7 5 *